SAMI'S
SLEEPAWAY
SUMMER

ALSO BY JENNY MEYERHOFF

Third Grade Baby
Playing Cupid

SAMI'S SLEEPAWAY SUMMER

By **Jenny Meyerhoff**
Illustrated by **Cathi Mingus**

SCHOLASTIC INC.

ISBN 978-0-545-33015-2
062130K3/B332/A8

2 2021

Printed in the U.S.A. 23

This edition first printing 2021
Designed by Yaffa Jaskoll
Illustrations by Cathi Mingus

*For Mom and Dad—thank you for sending me
to camp even though I cried.
And for Camp Ramah in Canada, thank you for
five magical summers.*

CHAPTER 1

YOU HAVE TO GO, BUT YOU DON'T HAVE TO LIKE IT

I tiptoe into my big sister Maya's bedroom, lie down on the floor, and slide under her bed. I'm hiding from my mother. Normally I'm not allowed to go into Maya's bedroom without permission, but Maya isn't here. She's at sleepaway camp. She's been gone for two weeks, and this is an emergency.

My mother wants me to go to camp, too. Tomorrow morning she's going to put me on a bus and send me to Camp Cedar Lake, where I don't know anyone (except for my sister). I will have to stay there for four whole days. Right now, she wants me to pack.

I figure if she can't find me, I can't pack, and if I can't pack, I can't go to camp. It's the perfect plan.

"Sami!" I hear my mother's voice in the hallway. "Sami, where are you?"

I slide further under the bed until something fuzzy brushes my arm. I almost scream before I realize it's just Mrs. Parsley, Maya's stuffed bunny. I guess Maya forgot to bring her to camp. Ever since Maya started seventh grade, she's been forgetting a lot of things. She forgot that we always see Disney movies together, and she went to see the new princess movie with her friends. She forgot that we find the *afikomen* together at Passover and share the prize. This year she found it alone and kept the whole five dollars to herself. She also forgot that she promised she would write to me every single day of camp. She's only sent me one e-mail so far.

"Samantha Ruth Bloom!" Mom calls. "If you don't come right now, I'm going to pack for you myself, and then you'll just have to wear the clothes I pick, even if you don't like them."

I sigh and slide myself out from under Maya's bed. I didn't think about the fact that Mom could pack for me. There just doesn't seem to be any way out of camp. I should know. I've been trying to get out of it for weeks.

"Coming!" I call. Then I lay Mrs. Parsley on the bed so she won't have to sit in the dust for six more weeks.

My mom walks into the room, her brown hair held back by a headband, same as mine. She is holding a pale blue duffel bag and a piece of paper, which she hands to me.

"The packing list," she says. My mom isn't usually the kind of mom who makes her kids do stuff they're scared of, like trying new foods or ordering at a restaurant all by ourselves, but for some reason, she wants me to go to camp.

I scan the list and see mostly what I expected: sunscreen, bug spray, T-shirts, and bathing suits.

"*Six* pairs of underwear?" I ask. "Why do I need so many?"

Mom spreads the open duffel bag on the floor. "I'm not sure. Better safe than sorry?"

I don't really see how extra underwear can make me feel safe, and I'm already sorry.

Every time I think about going to sleepaway camp, it gives me *shpilkes*. That's a word I learned in the Yiddish class I take at my synagogue with my grandma.

Not all Jewish people speak Yiddish. Most of us don't, but Grandma thought it would be fun. And it is. I'd rather say *shpilkes* than "nervous wiggles."

"How many pairs of shorts do you need?" Mom asks, pulling open my dresser drawer.

I check the list. "Four. And one pair of jeans," I say. "Also, I'm supposed to bring my own canoe so I can paddle myself home early if I really hate it."

Mom laughs. "There's no river between Cedar Lake, Wisconsin, and Highland Park, Illinois, Sami. Besides, you're going to love Camp Cedar

Lake once you get there. It's completely normal to feel anxious before you go."

I fold my arms across my chest. "I'm not going to love it."

Mom gives me a look. "Sami, I don't want to fight about this again. Camp Cedar Lake is important to our family. It's where your dad and I met. Uncle Brad and Aunt Jamie went there, too. Maya was terrified her first summer and now she loves it! Plus, it's just mini-camp for now."

"I know, I know." I sigh. Cedar Lake Mini-Camp is a four-day, three-night miniature version of regular camp. But even though it's shorter, it still has all the tortures of regular camp.

Mom stands up and kisses my forehead. "I'm going to get your towels and sheets from the dryer. Will you finish loading your clothes?"

I nod to my mom as she walks out my door. "I bet when we pick you up from camp on Sunday, you'll be begging to stay," she calls back over her shoulder.

That won't happen. "Remember our deal," I answer.

This is our deal: I will give mini-camp a fair try, and if I don't like it, I won't have to go back ever again. I already know I won't like it. I'm not a sleepaway camp kind of kid, and you just can't change who you are.

I pick up the stack of T-shirts from my dresser and put them into my duffel bag.

Reason number one that I'm not a sleepaway camp kind of kid: I'm allergic to nature. No, *really*. Whenever I step outside in my bare feet, my left ear itches like crazy.

I pick up a stack of shorts and pack them next to the stack of T-shirts.

Reason number two that I'm not a sleepaway camp kind of kid: I like quiet activities, like making up songs. At camp you have to do things like tubing and ropes course. I read it on the Camp Cedar Lake website.

I will never, ever do the ropes course. Heights

are not my friend. Two weeks ago I went to Speedworld Amusement Park for my cousin Daniel's birthday party, and I was so scared when I went on the roller coaster that I barfed in my mouth. Then I had to spend the rest of the day with my four-year-old cousin Chloe at the Zippy Zoomers Kiddie Pad.

I will never do another high-up activity ever again. However, according to the Camp Cedar Lake website, camp is full of high-up activities.

After I'm all packed up, Mom tells me to put on a dress because it is time for a special good-bye dinner with Grandma. Here are the people I like who are attending the dinner: me, Mom, Dad, Grandma, Aunt Jamie, Uncle Brad, and Chloe. Here are the people I do not like who are attending the dinner: my cousin Daniel. Daniel is the very same age I am, and you would think that since we are both nine and we both have the last name Bloom, it would be easy for us to get along.

You would think that, but you would be wrong.

In my opinion, Daniel is a *nudnik*. That's another word I learned in my Yiddish class. It means "an annoying person," and that fits Daniel perfectly. By the way, Daniel is in my Yiddish class. Grandma takes it with both of us, because she wants us to become best friends. She always says, "Having a same-age cousin is a very special thing. You might not realize it now, but when you *really* need someone, you'll always have each other. There's no substitute for *mish-pucha*."

Mishpucha means "family," and it's definitely my grandmother's favorite Yiddish word. I like it, too, except for when it comes to *nudnik* Daniel. When the teacher taught us the word *nudnik*, Daniel did not even notice that the word was made for him.

Reason number one that Daniel is a *nudnik*: He thinks he knows everything.

Reason number two that Daniel is a *nudnik*: He always has to be the best at everything.

Reason number three that Daniel is a *nudnik*: He calls me Samantha.

When we get to Café Italia, I want to sit between my parents, but Daniel says, "Sit next to me, *Samantha*, so I can tell you about camp."

"Sami," I mumble, but Daniel ignores me.

"You two are going to have so much fun together!" Grandma says.

All the grown-ups agree with her, so I sit down with Daniel on my left side and Dad on my right. Dad hands me a children's menu.

"I order from the grown-up menu," Daniel says when my dad tries to pass him a children's menu.

"Daniel has such a sophisticated palate," Aunt Jamie explains. "The other day I asked him what he wanted for lunch and he said, 'Chopped liver.'"

All the grown-ups laugh. I glance over at Daniel, and he's practically ready to stand up and take a bow.

"I want chopped liver, too," Chloe says. "What's chopped liver?"

The grown-ups laugh again, but not as much as before.

"*You* wouldn't like it, Chloe," Daniel says. "You're a picky eater."

He says the words *picky eater* like they mean "revolting slime monster." Chloe's face falls. I guess I'm lucky Daniel is only my cousin.

"Don't worry, Chloe," I say. "I'm a picky eater, too."

"What are you going to do at camp?" Daniel asks me. "I doubt they are going to serve grilled cheese at every meal."

For a second my heart stops beating. What *am* I going to do at camp? I've been so busy worrying about nature and heights that I forgot to worry about food.

Reason number three that I'm not a sleepaway camp kind of kid: I only like eleven foods.

"Here's what you should do," Daniel says.

"Just try one new food at each meal. By the end of the weekend, you won't be picky anymore."

I don't bother explaining to Daniel that the reason I'm picky is that whenever I think about trying new foods, my stomach squeezes into a ball and I lose my appetite. If it was easy for me to try new foods, I wouldn't be picky.

"Good idea," I say instead.

"I know," he answers, nodding at me.

I have to give mini-camp a fair try, but thank goodness I don't have to give Daniel a fair try, too.

That night, as I lie in bed trying to fall asleep, I'm so anxious that even my *shpilkes* have *shpilkes*. I reach under my pillow for the e-mail Maya sent me—the *only* e-mail Maya sent me. Mom printed it out. The paper is soft and wrinkly, because I've already read it about a hundred times, but I think I need to read it again. It's the only thing that calms me down when my camp *shpilkes* start.

Dear Samsters!

Camp is awesome as usual. There is a new girl in my cabin this year. She is really nice but really home-sick. I taught her your special cheer-up cure. Remember that song you wrote to the tune of "Yankee Doodle"?

Farshtinkener, farshtinkener,
farshtinkener, farshtunken.
Farshtinkener, farshtinkener,
farshtinkener, farshtunken!

I guess you did learn something cool in that Yiddish class. I don't know if it cured her homesickness, but it made us laugh, so thanks!

I know you're feeling worried about camp, but after a few days, everyone here will seem like family! It's a home away from home. No sister of mine could possibly dislike camp. Especially when we celebrate Shabbat. It's magical!

Anyway, I can't wait for you to come up here! I promise I'll be waiting for you the second you get off the bus. We'll hang out all the time and I'll show you the ropes. And the ropes course! (Everybody does it, and everybody loves it!)

XOXOXO,

Maya

P.S. I taught my cabin your Camp Cedar Lake song yesterday at rest hour. They think it's hysterical! But we're going to have to do something about those lyrics.

P.P.S. This year my cabin is taking a canoe trip around Skeleton Lake!! I hope it's not haunted.

I fold the paper up but don't stick it under my pillow. Maybe if I hold on to it while I sleep, it'll help me feel less scared. I won't be at camp alone, I remind myself. Maya will be there. She'll hang out with me the whole time. She promised. It'll be just like home, only with more trees.

I close my eyes and sing the Camp Cedar Lake song I wrote to the tune of "America the Beautiful." (That's the one that starts "O beautiful for spacious skies.") The lyrics seem fine to me.

> *"Camp Cedar Lake,*
> *So far away,*
> *I've traveled all alone.*
> *To make new friends*
> *I will not try.*
> *I'd rather be at home.*
> *Camp Cedar Lake, Camp Cedar Lake,*
> *Your trees so big and tall.*
> *They make me sneeze. You're full of fleas.*
> *I don't like you at all."*

I hum the last line, because I'm too tired to sing. Then I fall asleep and dream that all the cabins are tree houses hanging a hundred feet in the air.

CHAPTER 2

TRY NOT TO SIT NEXT
TO YOUR COUSIN
ON THE BUS

The first thing I hear when I climb out of my parents' minivan is "Samantha! You almost missed the bus! What took you guys so long?"

We are in the parking lot of Deerfield High School. That's where parents take their kids to meet the bus that will drive them to Camp Cedar Lake. The camp website said to arrive at nine A.M. It is 9:01.

Daniel runs over to me with his parents following. Uncle Brad is holding Chloe. She's still in her pj's, holding her blankie and sucking her thumb. She gets to go back home.

"Didn't you get any Camp Cedar Lake gear?" Daniel asks me. He is wearing a Camp Cedar Lake baseball cap, a Camp Cedar Lake T-shirt, and Camp Cedar Lake shorts, and he has a Camp Cedar Lake sweatshirt tied around his waist.

"Maya told me she'd give me one of her old shirts," I say.

"Oh," he says, nodding.

"But she forgot," I add softly.

Daniel's eyebrows wrinkle. "I'm sure you'll be fine without one," he says, but his voice doesn't sound like he means it.

I scan the parking lot, and it seems like everyone is wearing brand-new Camp Cedar Lake clothes. I'm wearing my *Shrek the Musical* T-shirt. If Camp Cedar Lake clothing was a requirement, they should have said that on the website. How can I like a camp that forgets to tell me something so important? Everything important in life should be on a website—that's my new motto.

"That's where we check in," Dad announces,

pointing to a gray-haired lady in a Camp Cedar Lake visor. "Let's go."

As we are walking over, my mother's phone beeps. She checks it and says, "An e-mail from Maya!"

Mom stops to read the e-mail while I follow Dad to the check-in lady, but I don't really listen to anything she tells us. I'm too busy worrying about what else they forgot to put on the website.

"Let's head to the bus," Daniel says after the lady finishes putting check marks by our names. "I want to get the best seats, right in front."

There doesn't seem to be a good way to tell Daniel that I'd rather sit by myself, so before I know it, I'm crammed next to him in the aisle seat of the third row on the bus. My dad and Daniel's parents, with Chloe, crowd around us. Other kids squeeze past them to claim their seats. My eyes are starting to feel prickly. I don't want to cry in front of Daniel, but I'm not sure I'm going to have a choice.

Then Mom climbs onto the bus.

"Sami," she says, "I have to tell you something."

Her face is very serious, and my *shpilkes* know that that is a terrible sign.

"I just read Maya's e-mail. She is very sorry, but her cabin is leaving on an overnight trip this morning. She's not going to be at camp when you get there."

"But . . . but . . ." I don't believe it. Maya *promised*. "But I'll be all alone," I say.

"No you won't, silly," Aunt Jamie says. "You'll have Daniel."

I think my thoughts as loud as I can, hoping my mother will hear them: *I don't want Daniel. I want my sister.*

"Can't Maya skip the overnight?" I ask.

My mother tilts her head and makes a sad face. "That wouldn't be fair to Maya, sweetie. She wants to enjoy this experience with her cabin."

My heart is racing. I don't want to go to camp

if Maya won't be with me. What about what's fair to me?

"Maya wrote a message for you," Mom says. "You can read it."

She pulls out her phone and shows it to me.

Don't worry, Samsters. Even though I'm not actually there, you'll still know I'm thinking about you every second, promise! Besides, before long the girls in your cabin are going to seem like sisters. Mine do! You'll probably even get to know them better without me in the way. And I'll come say hi to you as soon as I get back to camp, I triple promise! I'll be back by Shabbat.

I hand the phone back to my mom. I'm sick of Maya's promises. The bus driver turns on the motor and makes an announcement over the loudspeaker. "Okay, everyone, it's time for final good-byes. One last hug, then everyone who isn't going to camp needs to exit the bus. Thank you for your cooperation."

My heart lurches into my mouth and a tear slides down my cheek.

Daniel's parents hug him good-bye and climb off the bus. Mom hugs me and squeezes my hand. "It'll be okay," she says. "I promise. By the time camp is over, you'll probably wish you could stay forever."

I give Mom a "no way" look.

"Last call," the bus driver says.

Dad gives me one more hug. "You're going to do great!" he says. I wish I could believe him.

My parents exit the bus and it feels like my heart is leaving with them. The rumble of the engine echoes in my chest. I know they are part of the crowd standing in the parking lot waving good-bye, but since Daniel took the window seat, I can't see them at all. Then I find them. My father has his arm wrapped around my mother, who has her head resting against his shoulder. There is something funny about her face. I scoot onto my knees and peer over Daniel's head so I can get a better look.

My mother is crying!

Crying? That is not a good sign. Why would she send me someplace that makes her cry? I am about to run off the bus and tell my parents they can forget about camp when the doors whoosh closed and the bus rolls away from the crowd.

"Camp Cedar Lake," the driver says into the loudspeaker. "Ready or not, here we come!"

Oy vey.

My chin wobbles, so I hunch away from Daniel. I don't need to spend the entire ride listening to him tell me how easy it is *not* to be homesick. I recline my seat and close my eyes. Even though the noise of the bus and all the kids talking is really loud, maybe I can fall asleep for four days and not wake up until it's time to go home.

Daniel has other ideas. He taps me on the shoulder.

"Do you know how to play spit?" he asks, taking out a pack of cards. "It's the perfect game to play during rest hour."

21

I turn my body to face him and sigh. "No," I say. "I don't."

"Oh. Well, how about spoons? Do you know that one?"

I bite my lip. "Uh-uh."

"Do you at least know crazy eights? War? Go fish?" Daniel shakes his head at me and tsks. "Okay, it might take the whole ride, but I'm going to teach them to you."

That's the last thing I want to do on the bus ride! "Maya says the girls in her cabin play jacks, Chinese jump rope, and cat's cradle."

Daniel gives me a look like he's not sure he should believe me. "I've never heard of those. Did Maya teach you how to play them?"

My eyes start to feel all prickly again. Maya didn't teach me. She said she would, but she forgot. I shake my head.

"Trust me," Daniel says as he starts dealing the cards. "I'm sure more people play spit."

Spit is the fastest, most confusing card game

in the world. Daniel tries to teach me for about twenty minutes before he gives up, saying, "You should probably just read a book during rest hour."

I don't answer him, because between the nature, the heights, the food, Maya's camping trip, and now the rest hour games, my brain is so full of worries it doesn't have any energy left for speaking. Daniel and I sit quietly while a counselor with blond curly hair begins to walk down the aisle of the bus, counting campers. He taps me lightly on the head, then taps Daniel, then moves on. Doesn't he realize he should have counted us before the bus left?

I pull out my notebook, thinking I might try to write a song, an I-can't-wait-to-go-home song, but Daniel interrupts me.

"What activities are you most excited about?"

I'm not really excited about anything, but Daniel answers his own question before I can tell him that.

"I'm most excited for everything having to do with water. Swimming, of course, since I'm Red Cross level 6B. Also tubing, canoeing, sailing, and windsurfing. My mom signed me up for private lessons in all of them before camp so I would know what I was doing and wouldn't completely embarrass myself the first time out."

Three of Daniel's words echo in my head. *Completely embarrass myself, completely embarrass myself, completely embarrass myself.*

Great! Now I have another thing to worry about.

"So what are your best activities?" Daniel asks.

"My *best* activities?" How can I have any best ones? Camp hasn't even started.

"You know, activities that you want to earn a Cedar Badge in."

Ha! Finally I know something Daniel doesn't know.

"You can't earn any badges at mini-camp," I say. "That takes a whole session or even more."

Daniel shakes his head at me in a way that makes my *shpilkes* do the hula.

"My mom called Rabbi Joe, the camp director," he says, as though I don't know exactly who Rabbi Joe is. "He's giving me special permission to do a Cedar Swim."

My jaw drops. A Cedar Swim is when you swim all the way around Cedar Lake. It's the thing you do to earn a Cedar Badge in swimming. Maya didn't do it until her second year of camp.

"I want to be the youngest camper ever to earn a badge," Daniel says.

I open my notebook and start scribbling a song.

(To the tune of "Clementine")
Oh my cousin, oh my cousin,
Oh my cousin, you nudnik,
I am tired of your questions
And you make me feel quite sick.

"What are you writing?" Daniel asks, peering over my shoulder.

"Nothing." I slam my notebook closed. "Just a song."

"You write songs?" His eyes widen, and I can tell he's surprised.

"Yep," I say. "I even wrote one about Camp Cedar Lake. Want to hear it?" I chuckle on the inside, because I know he won't like my camp song. But that's what's so perfect about it.

"Sure," he says. "But do you know any of the *real* songs? I memorized the words from the website, but my mom didn't know the tunes."

I do know them. That's the one thing Maya taught me. But those songs are for people who like camp—which I don't.

"My song is better," I tell Daniel. "Trust me. Before the weekend is over, I bet all the kids at mini-camp will be singing it."

"Really?" Daniel looks impressed. It almost makes me like him a little bit. "Will you teach me? I could help you teach the other campers. My music teacher at school says I have perfect pitch."

I groan. "It's to the tune of—"

A loud guitar strum blasting through the bus speakers cuts me off. The man with the blond curly hair has the bus walkie-talkie clipped to the neck of his CAMP CEDAR LAKE STAFF T-shirt, and he's sitting on the edge of his seat with a guitar in his lap. He stands and faces the back of the bus.

"Okay, Cedar Lake campers!" His voice is full of enthusiasm and I smile, because I can't help myself. "My name is Howie, and I'm the C.C.L. song leader!"

A bunch of kids say, "Hi, Howie," in singsong voices.

"I can't hear you!" he says.

"Hi, Howie!" they shout.

"That's better!" Howie winks at us. "Singing is a big part of Camp Cedar Lake, so I thought I'd teach you a few songs to help us pass the time on the bus. Sound good?"

Everyone cheers and Howie picks out a few notes with his fingers. The vibrations hum through me. Some of the Camp Cedar Lake songs are pretty nice. I think it would be okay to sing them on the bus as long as I don't sing them once I get to camp. Then I would be able to tell my mom I gave singing a fair try.

"Okay, this first song is a new one. One of our fifth-year campers wrote it. I'll sing it first. Then we'll go through line by line."

I'm a little surprised to hear he's teaching us a song written by a camper. They never mentioned on the website that campers could write camp songs. I mean, it doesn't matter anyway, since I'm not a sleepaway camp kind of kid. But still, it would have been nice to know.

I think somebody should have a talk with Rabbi Joe about his website.

CHAPTER 3

TOP BUNKS
ARE TROUBLE

Howie teaches us a bunch more songs. Then finally he says, "That's it for now, campers. We've only got about a half an hour left of the bus ride. You'll know we're getting close to camp when you see the cedar trees lining the road. Keep your eyes open!"

"I'm lucky I have perfect song memory," Daniel says to me. "Did you know that, Samantha?"

"Sami," I grumble.

He ignores me. "Okay, teach me your song."

I open my mouth to sing, but Daniel grabs my arm.

"Wait!" he says. "I have a great idea. Howie! Howie!"

The song leader peers over the back of his seat at us. "Yeee-ehsss?" he says in a slow and silly way.

"Sami wrote a song about Camp Cedar Lake," Daniel tells him. "We want to teach it to the other kids on the bus."

"Do you?" He raises one eyebrow and makes a funny face at us, like he's a detective sizing us up. "Let me hear it."

I shift around in my seat. Singing my song for Daniel is not the same as singing it for Howie. Why did Daniel have to tell Howie we wanted to teach it? It's my song anyway, not mine and Daniel's!

"You won't like it," I tell Howie.

"If you wrote it, I'm sure I'll love it," he tells me. "I have a special place in my heart for all the Cedar Lake songwriters."

"Okay." I sing them my song. Daniel looks like

he wants to bop me on the head with his backpack.

"Sorry," he says to Howie. "She told me she wrote a *real* song."

"It's a real song," I say.

Howie nods at me. "It's a real sad song," he says. "I'm not sure it's right for the other campers. But maybe someday you'll want to change the words."

I shake my head. I doubt it.

Reason number one that I will never change the words to my song: I'm not a sleepaway camp kind of kid. And you can't change who you are.

Reason number two that I will never change the words to my song: If you can't change who you are, then you can't change what you wrote. That's my songwriting motto.

"Cedar trees!" someone shouts. Everyone on the bus rushes to the windows on the left—everyone except me. And Daniel, he's staring at me angrily.

"You didn't have to embarrass me," he says.

"You're the one who made me sing for Howie," I remind him.

"Yeah, well, I thought you'd have a normal song. Everyone in our family is supposed to love Camp Cedar Lake."

"Not me," I tell him. "I'll never like camp."

For the last few minutes of the drive, the bus travels over a gravel road, and Daniel and I get bounced and jostled into each other about a thousand times. That makes it hard for us to ignore each other, but we do our best. Then the bus pulls into camp. Ahead of us a large green field spreads out under a pure blue sky. A dirt road circles the field, and towering cedar trees circle the road.

When I look closer, I can see buildings nestled in the cedar forest. I pick out the ones I recognize from the website: the rows of cabins, the mess hall, the arts and crafts shack. As I climb from the bus, I see kids everywhere. A group of teenagers with towels hanging over their shoulders walks by us. I watch them head to a place where sparkling blue water twinkles at me from between the leaves. I can just see a soft, sandy beach at the end of the path. Cedar Lake!

I take a deep breath, and the pine scent is the nicest smell I've ever inhaled. I feel like I'm standing in a postcard. I've seen pictures of camp before, some taken by Maya and some on the website, but in person Camp Cedar Lake is the most beautiful place ever. I turn around to look at the green forest behind me, but what I see makes my heart fall out of my chest. Rising high above the treetops, the ropes course sways in the breeze, reminding me that no matter how pretty this place is, I'll never be a sleepaway camp kind of kid.

All the new campers stand in the field next to the bus, and Daniel moves himself as far away from me as possible. Good.

A group of grown-ups stands in front of us,

and one of them, wearing a backward baseball hat and a Beatles T-shirt, takes a step forward. "Welcome to Camp Cedar Lake!" he says. "I'm Rabbi Joe."

"Hi, Rabbi Joe," everyone but me answers.

"We are very excited to have you all with us for the next four days and to show you why Camp Cedar Lake is the most special camp on earth. Standing next to me are your counselors. Each and every one of them started out at mini-camp when they were your age. This might be you someday."

Rabbi Joe gives us a big smile, but I don't smile back. It will not be me. I won't even be coming back next year.

"If you are a nine-year-old girl," he says, "meet Yael and Becca."

I snap to attention. Two teenage girls with brown hair, straight on one and wavy on the other, step forward. "I am Yael," the straight-haired one says with an accent. I realize she must be from Israel. "We are in Cabin Shemesh, the sun cabin. All the cabins are named for things in nature. Okay, now follow me!"

"Don't worry about your duffel bags," Becca adds. "Someone will bring them by later."

I gulp and, along with five other girls, follow Yael and Becca. Four of the girls start introducing themselves to one another. They walk bunched up in a group, giggling. The other girl, who has pale blond hair with bangs, walks quietly next to the counselors. I trail behind them all.

Here is the thing I like about my cabin: It has bathrooms. Maya said some of the cabins don't have bathrooms and you have to walk to the shower house every time you have to go.

Here is the thing I do not like about my cabin: It has bunk beds. That means there is a 50 percent chance I will have to sleep high up in the air. I do not want to sleep high up in the air.

Each set of bunk beds is labeled with two sun-shaped name tags. I find my name and realize

I'm bunkmates with the blond girl. Her name is Gabby.

"Hi. I'm Sami," I say, pointing to my name tag. "I guess we're bunkmates."

Gabby smiles and nods. "I'm G-G-Gabby," she says. I notice she's wearing a long thread around her neck that has a small notepad dangling from it.

"So, do you want the top bunk or the bottom bunk?" I ask her.

Gabby points to the top bunk but raises her eyebrows and tilts her head like she's asking me if I want it, too.

I shake my head. "No! I want the bottom bunk."

Gabby beams and tosses her backpack on her bed. Then she climbs up after it and bounces on her knees a couple of times. I guess she doesn't like to talk much because of her stutter. That proves that Maya was totally wrong about the girls in my cabin. How can I be friends with someone who doesn't like to talk, especially when singing is my favorite thing in the world?

Gabby waves me up to join her on the top bunk. I shake my head. The bunk bed is taller than I am. No way am I going up there.

Gabby waves me up again, like she *really* wants me to join her.

"I don't like heights," I tell her, but her only answer is to wave me up again.

I sigh. It's really hard to have an argument with a girl who barely talks. I have a feeling that if I don't go up there, she'll just wave at me all afternoon. I drop my backpack on my own bed and start to climb up the ladder. I keep my eyes straight ahead and don't look down.

When I reach the mattress, my hands hurt from holding on so tight. Gabby scoots over to make room for me and pats the bed, but I shake my head. I stay in the corner, where I can hold on to the rail and keep my legs on the ladder just in case. You should always have something to hold on to. That's my bunk-bed motto.

Gabby taps my shoulder and points out at

the cabin. I look around and finally see what people must like about top bunks. The cabin looks totally different from up here: bigger and smaller at the same time. You can see everything, the entire room, but not the way you see it when you're on the ground. Here you're above it, apart, just looking at it. It's kind of cool until one of our cabinmates walks by and accidentally bumps the corner of the bed. I scream and hug the rail as tight as I can.

Everyone freezes and stares at me. Great! Now everyone in my cabin thinks I'm a big *nebbish*. I can see them looking at one another. They must be glad they don't have to be bunkmates with the cabin dork.

I take a deep breath and remind myself it doesn't matter. After this weekend, I won't have to see any of them ever again. Now I can tell my mom I gave bunk beds a fair try.

"*Kol beseder?* Everything okay?" Yael walks over and rubs my knee.

"Yeah, I'm fine. I thought I was going to fall." I turn my body around and climb down the ladder. "I guess I'm a bottom bunk kind of kid."

Gabby makes a wrinkly forehead face like she feels sorry for me, and Yael squeezes my shoulder. "That just means that you two are perfect bunkmates: one who loves the top and one who loves the bottom," Yael says. "Your fairy campmothers were right when they told me to put you together."

"Our fairy campmothers?" I ask.

Gabby grabs her pad and writes Fairy camp-mothers?

Yael winks at us. "That's just what I call them."

"But who are they?" I ask. I don't know any mothers at camp. Did my mom and grandma call Yael? But they don't know Gabby.

"They are two people who want the girls in our cabin to have the best four days of their lives. But I'll never tell their names!" Yael says. "It's a mystery you have to solve for yourselves."

She leaves just as Howie drops a big pile of duffel bags on the front porch of our cabin.

"Okay, everyone," Becca announces. "Let's get our clothes into our cubbies and our sheets onto our beds. Then it'll be time for a cabin meeting!"

I get right to work putting everything away. I ask Gabby if she has any guesses about the fairy campmothers, but she shakes her head. It really is a mystery!

CHAPTER 4

**DON'T SIT IN
THE GRASS**

After we finish unpacking, my cabin gathers at the edge of the big field. Becca tells us all to sit on the grass. Sitting on the grass is like walking barefoot on the grass with your entire legs instead of just your feet. Not only is my left ear itching like crazy, but my *tukhus* itches, too. *Tukhus* is one of my favorite Yiddish words. It means "rear end." When the teacher taught it to us, Daniel and I looked at each other and burst out laughing. It's the only time I remember ever cracking up with my cousin.

Anyway, *tukhuses* are funny, but not when

they're itchy. I hope we don't have to sit in the grass for a long time. At least I can tell my mom I gave sitting in the grass a fair try.

Yael hands a bubble-gum-filled lollipop to every girl in my cabin. "Your fairy campmothers left these treats for you, for a sweet beginning." She winks at me as she says this. "They want you to know that you may feel like strangers today, but before long you are going to feel like family."

I put my lollipop on the grass without unwrapping it. I don't need any more family. I already have a sister who breaks her promises and a cousin who is a *nudnik*. That's plenty.

I lean my chin into my hand and sigh while Yael and Becca pass out CEDAR LAKE MINI-CAMP T-shirts to all of us.

Gabby taps me on the shoulder. "W-what's wr-wrong?"

I shrug but sit up and try to smile. "I don't like sitting on grass," I tell her.

Gabby giggles. I guess it is kind of funny. "It

makes my *tukhus* itch," I explain, and Gabby giggles even more.

"Okay," Yael says when the T-shirts are all passed out. "Let's start with a get-to-know-you game."

Becca explains. "I'll say my name and something I like that starts with the same letter as my name. Then the next person will repeat what I said and add to it with her own name and something she likes. Does that make sense?"

Everyone nods and Becca begins. "My name is Becca, and I like bagels."

Yael goes next. "Her name is Becca and she likes bagels. My name is Yael and I like yaks. Who wants to go next?"

A dark-haired girl named Isabelle raises her hand and the game continues until finally it's my turn. I'm the second-to-last person. I take a deep breath and try to remember what everyone said. "Becca likes bagels. Yael likes yaks. Isabelle likes her iPod. Reese likes Reese's peanut butter cups.

Lily likes llamas, and Ella likes *everything*. My name is Sami. I like singing."

I turn to Gabby and my stomach twists. How will she manage to play the game? She gives everyone a wobbly smile. It's the first time I've seen her look scared.

Yael leans over and says softly, "Just do whatever you feel comfortable doing."

"M-m-m—" Gabby stops, and her face pinches as though she's hurt. The other girls in the circle start to fidget and look away. Some of them even cover their mouths like they might be laughing. I wish I could do something to help Gabby.

"Her name is Gab—" I start, but Becca stops me.

"It's okay, Sami."

Gabby takes a deep breath and tries again. "M-m-m—"

She stops. Then she lifts her notepad. She writes something on it, then holds it up for all to see: My name is Gabby. I like games.

"I bet you'll have a bunch of good ones to teach us at rest hour," Yael says.

Gabby nods really fast.

"I can't wait to learn them," Yael says.

"But she didn't say the rest of our names," Isabelle says. "That's not fair."

"Yeah," says Lily.

I see Isabelle's point, but it also doesn't seem fair to make Gabby say all the names.

"She's fine," Becca says in a firm voice. I glance at Gabby. Her cheeks are bright red. She writes something in her notepad really quickly.

"If Gabby doesn't want to say, or write, all the names she doesn't have to," Yael says softly. "We won't make anyone do anything that makes them feel uncomfortable."

Gabby looks up and opens her mouth, but no sound comes out. I don't think anyone notices but me.

"Okay?" says Becca. "Let's move on with our meeting."

Suddenly I realize what Gabby's doing.

"Wait," I say and everyone's eyes turn to me. "Gabby didn't finish her turn."

"Sami," Yael says softly. "She doesn't have to—"

"She wants to." I point to Gabby's notebook, and she holds it up.

Becca — bagels
Yael — yaks
Isabelle — iPods
Reese — Reese's cups
Lily — llamas
Ella — everything
Sami — singing

"Hers was the hardest," I tell everyone. "She had to remember all our names."

"You're right," says Yael. "*Mazel tov*, Gabby."

I laugh and say *mazel tov*, too. So do Reese and Ella.

"Okay, now for the fun part." Becca stands and

holds up a poster board decorated with drawings of cedar trees and stars and sailboats and shining suns. In the middle is a list of all the things we will do for the entire weekend. "This is our schedule."

Yael and Becca take turns reading the schedule to us. Here are the activities that don't sound too bad: arts and crafts, music, and canoeing. Here is the activity that sounds terrible: ropes course. No way, no how! Never let your feet leave the ground if they don't have to. That's my activities motto.

"We'll be doing all these activities with the nine-year-old boys' cabin, Cabin Kochavim, the star cabin," Yael adds. "If it says two activities, like archery and animal care, it means you have a choice."

"It might seem like a lot now," Becca adds, "but it's going to go by so fast you won't believe it!"

I *don't* believe it. I've only been at camp for an hour, and it already feels like days!

"Okay!" Yael says. "Let's go to lunch."

After rest hour, Becca tells us to change into our bathing suits. It is time for free swim.

We have to change in the cabin, where everyone can see everything. I've never changed in front of anyone besides my family before. I pull my bathing suit out of my cubby but just hold it tightly for a while.

Everyone else is standing around holding their suits, too. I bet we are all wondering the same thing: Will we look like chickens if we try to change in the bathroom instead of the middle of the cabin? I miss being at home, where I have my own room and can change in complete privacy.

"Girls, unless you want to swim in your underwear, I suggest you get into your suits," Becca says with a wink. "We're leaving in one minute! Yael and I will be waiting on the porch."

Even after our counselors leave, we all just stand around, frozen. No one wants to be the first to start changing. Finally Gabby says, "I h-have a b-b-b-bikini. I n-never w-wore it before." She holds up a white top with pink polka dots, but none of the girls answer her. I see Isabelle and Lily exchanging bulgy-eye looks, like they are making fun. It makes my stomach hurt.

"I never wore a bikini, either!" I tell her. "But I only wear two-piece bathing suits. Otherwise it's too hard to go to the bathroom."

Gabby laughs, and so does Ella.

"I have a tankini," I say, holding up my blue and green tie-dye suit.

"Me too," says Reese. She holds up a silver metallic suit.

"Want to hear the bathing suit song I just made up?" I ask them. "It's to the tune of 'She'll Be Coming Round the Mountain.'"

"Sure," Reese says. I don't wait for the other girls to answer. I just start singing.

"Oh I never wore a bi-ki-ni before.
Oh I never wore a bi-ki-ni before.

But I always wear a two-piece,
Yes, I always wear a two-piece.
If I don't,
I might be peeing on the floor."

When I finish, there is total silence, and I worry my song was too weird. But then they all start laughing, even Isabelle and Lily. Suddenly it's as if no one feels uncomfortable anymore, and we all start changing into our bathing suits and singing my song.

"I have a bikini, too," Isabelle tells Gabby.

"Am I the only one with a one-piece?" Lily asks.

"B-be c-careful!" Gabby jokes.

"It's not a problem," Lily says. "I just pee in the lake, anyway."

"Eeew!" we all say.

"Kidding!" Lily laughs.

When we get to the beach, Daniel's cabin, Cabin Kochavim, is waiting for us. The head swim instructor tells us that after we pass a swim test, we can swim anywhere inside the buoys. We can also use the water trampoline, the slide, and a giant yellow puffball called the Blob.

We follow the instructor down the dock to the deep water, where we will have to swim two laps.

"Daniel Bloom?" The instructor looks around at all of us.

"Here!" Daniel's hand shoots up from the other end of the group.

"You can go with Anne," the head instructor says, pointing at another swim instructor.

"You're not going to swim with us?" one of Daniel's cabinmates asks.

"I'm doing a Cedar Swim," Daniel tells him. He waits a second, like he expects applause or something.

"Oh," his cabinmate says. "Wow. Good luck."

Daniel walks toward Anne, which means he has to walk past me.

"Excuse me," he says, even though I'm not in his way.

I move to the right, but he steps right, too. So I move left, but so does he. We keep trying to get out of each other's way, but keep stepping right back into each other's path. Finally I step way over, but my foot misses the edge of the dock and I land in the water.

When I come up spluttering, Daniel's face is bright red. He won't even look at me. I guess I must have embarrassed him again. I start to pull myself out of the water, but the head instructor says, "Stay in. You get to go first!"

Reason number one that I do not like to go first in swim tests: I only know one stroke—front crawl.

Reason number two that I do not like to go first in swim tests: I don't swim to the front. What I swim is more like diagonal crawl.

When I lift my head to take a breath, I realize I'm far, far away from the swim test area. I straighten myself out and finish the test.

Reason number three that I do not like to go first in swim tests: When you get out of the water and have snot hanging from your nose, everyone is still standing on the dock. That means everyone sees it.

At home when we go to the pool, I usually just bring a book and read in a lounge chair. Camp doesn't even have lounge chairs.

After the test, I go sit on the beach, wrapped in my towel. I wish I had a book. I wish Maya hadn't broken her promise and was here to tell me that falling in the water, swimming in a diagonal, and having snot aren't so bad. But she isn't. She'd rather be with her cabin.

Gabby comes over and makes swimming motions with her arms.

I shake my head.

She nods and pulls me up by the hand. Next thing I know, Gabby and I are sitting on the Blob.

"What's supposed to happen?" I ask her. "Do we just sit here all day?"

Gabby points up to a big platform behind us, where Isabelle and Reese are standing. "W-wait," she says.

"One, two, three!" Reese and Isabelle shout, and then they jump. The second they hit the puffball, Gabby and I are launched high into the air. I scream at the top of my lungs, then hit the water *tukhus*-first.

I'm so surprised I burst out laughing, and I decide I'd better do it again, just so I can tell Mom I gave swimming a fair try. As I climb back onto the Blob, I'm starting to think that not all of camp is terrible. Some parts are even a tiny bit okay. But then I notice something in the distance, just over the treetops at the far end of camp: the ropes tower, with the ropes all wobbly and wiggly and high, high, high. Even though the water in Cedar Lake is nice and warm, I start to shiver.

CHAPTER 5

DON'T EAT THE TOFU SURPRISE

Tonight the evening program is a camp scavenger hunt. There are clues hidden in different places all around the camp, each one leading to the next. The first cabin to find the end of the trail wins a midnight ice-cream party.

We don't win. Cabin Mayim, the water cabin, does. After the winner is announced, we walk back to our cabin in the dark, with Yael and Becca trailing behind us.

"I can't believe we got last place," Reese says as we climb up our front porch and head through the screen door. "Everyone has to promise to come back so we can win next year. I want that ice-cream party."

"I promise," says Lily.

"Me too," says Ella.

"And me," Isabelle adds.

Gabby puts out her pinky and all the other girls lock their pinkies around hers. They are hooked together in the center of the cabin, looking at me, waiting.

I'm standing by my lower bunk, holding my toothbrush and toothpaste. I start to feel the *shpilkes* again. If I was a sleepaway camp kind of kid, then I would want to be in their cabin. But I already decided. I'm not a sleepaway camp kind of kid.

"Time to get your pj's on." Yael walks through the cabin door. "It's almost time to say *lila tov*, good night."

"Just a few minutes until lights-out." Becca follows right behind her.

"I'm not even tired," Ella says.

"We were just in the middle of doing something," Reese adds.

"You'll have to finish up in the morning," Becca says, though her voice isn't mean. "You had a busy day and have to get up early tomorrow."

"If everyone is in bed in five minutes, I'll tell you a story about growing up in Israel," Yael adds.

The girls grumble, but unhook pinkies and start getting ready for bed. Only Gabby seems to remember that I never joined them. She walks over to me and sticks out her pinky. I shake my head and see the saddest face I've ever seen Gabby make.

"Sorry," I say. "I'm not a sleepaway camp kind of kid."

Gabby grabs my hand and nods vigorously. "Y-y-y—" She stops and takes a deep breath. I feel guilty because I'm making her talk.

"Sorry," I whisper, and suddenly a sadness as big as Cedar Lake fills the air all around me.

"I have to brush my teeth," I tell her, rushing off to the bathroom before my tears start falling.

I get ready for bed as quickly as possible. Then I climb into my bunk and pull the covers over my head so that no one will see me. The tears fall all through Yael's story. They soak my pillow, but I can't stop them.

Why didn't Maya skip her camping trip for me? Maybe she's embarrassed to have a sister who doesn't love camp. Maybe she's embarrassed to have a sister who wrote an I-don't-like-camp song. I remember the words from her first e-mail: *No sister of mine could possibly dislike camp.*

Maybe she just forgot about me, like she forgot Mrs. Parsley.

Suddenly I know I can't stay at camp another second. But how can I get Rabbi Joe to send me home?

I hold my breath to stop my tears and listen to the room. Yael finished her story a while ago, and now the cabin is quiet except for deep breathing and one person's snoring. I think it might be Ella. My stomach rumbles. All I had for dinner was a hot-dog bun.

Then it hits me! If I stay here, I'll starve. I'm sure it's against camp policy to let anyone starve. Maybe my parents can come right now. I slowly pull the covers off my face and sit up. Then I nearly have a heart attack. An upside-down head is floating in the air in front of me. "Ahhh!" I start to scream.

I cover my mouth with my hands when I realize it's Gabby, hanging over the edge of her bunk, watching me. She disappears for a second. Then I see her feet climbing down the ladder. She hops into bed with me and shows me a piece of paper from her notebook.

I know a song that will cheer you up.

"It's okay," I whisper. "You don't have to sing it. Nothing can cheer me up. I need to go home."

Gabby screws up her face and starts talking. "N-n-n—"

I put my hand out to stop her. "It's okay."

Gabby doesn't listen. She starts singing softly. *"Farshtinkener, farshtinkener, farshtinkener, farshtunken. Farshtinkener, farshtinkener, farshtin-kener, farshtunken!*" Gabby beams at me.

My heart stops.

"What?" I whisper before I realize I shouldn't ask her to talk again. I just can't believe it. "Never mind. I just . . . How did you know . . ." My brain can't figure out what I should say first. "You sang!"

"S-s-singing is easier," she says. "I l-love s-singing." Then she plugs her nose and waves her hand in front of her face like she smells something really stinky. "*Farshtinkener, farshtinkener,*" she sings again, giggling.

"But the song," I say. "That's my—"

I'm so confused. The only people who know "The Farshtinkener Song" are me, Maya, and my parents.

I look at Gabby. "S-sing," she says.

"*Farshtinkener, farshtinkener, farshtinkener, farshtunken.*" I start the song, and Gabby joins me halfway. We sing the rest together, keeping our voices as low as possible. Then I smile.

It's impossible for me to sing that song without smiling.

Gabby elbows me in the ribs and we smile again. "*F-farshtinkener*," she whispers. Her eyes light up as she says it. Then she pulls out her notepad and writes me a note: I practiced it at home, in case anyone was homesick.

How could she practice it at home? How did she even know it?

Camp is full of mysteries.

"P-please st-stay, S-Sami."

Gabby is holding my hand and looking at me with an expression that makes it impossible to ignore her. Besides, I don't feel as homesick as I did before.

"Okay," I whisper. I glance around the room at all my sleeping cabinmates. Just because I've decided to stay doesn't mean I changed my mind about camp. It's so I can tell my mom I gave it a fair try. And it's because I don't want to make Gabby sad.

I yawn. Then I yawn again. Crying is hard work. I lie down on my pillow and pull the covers up to my chin. "Good night."

"G-good n-night." Gabby climbs back up to her top bunk and waves at me over the side.

"Gabby?" I whisper.

She pokes her head over so she can see me.

"Thanks," I say. She nods, then disappears again.

When we wake up the next morning, Yael has another present for all of us.

"Your fairy campmothers were really busy getting ready for you to come to camp," she says. "They wish they could be here to give you these in person, but they can't, so they asked me to do it."

The fairy campmothers *again*?

Becca hands each of us a friendship bracelet. The bracelets are blue and white, Camp Cedar Lake colors.

"I know who the fairy campmothers are!" Ella

says. "It's you guys." She points to Yael and Becca.

"No," Yael says. "Not us."

"Then who?" I ask. "I don't know any old ladies."

Yael laughs. "They aren't really old. They just want to take care of all of you. So you feel good at camp."

"But why would they worry about us? We're total strangers."

"Maybe you are not total strangers." Yael winks again.

But we have to be. The only people I know at camp are Daniel and Maya. *They* can't be fairy campmothers. Daniel doesn't want to talk to me and Maya isn't here!

"We'd better get to services," Becca says. "Last one there has to stack the benches."

"I don't want to go to services," Isabelle says. She is still in her bottom bunk, listening to her iPod. "Services are a bunch of boring old men mumbling in Hebrew."

"Sorry, sweetie," Yael says, going over to her bed, grabbing Isabelle by the hand, and trying to pull her up. "We've all got to go. But I think you will be surprised what services are like at camp."

"Yep," Becca adds. "You've got to go. We do all our activities as a group. No one misses anything!"

Isabelle sighs and gets out of bed. We all laugh when we see she is already completely dressed.

"Oh well," she says. "It was worth a try."

After services—which remind me of a big sing-along (no boring old men anywhere)—we do breakfast and cabin cleanup. Then we meet Daniel's cabin at the waterfront for tubing and canoeing. The water-skiing instructor divides everyone into groups, but Anne, the swim instructor, pulls Daniel aside.

"Daniel," one of his cabinmates calls. "Aren't you going to go tubing with us?"

"I'm going to do the Cedar Swim," he says.

"Again?" his cabinmate asks. "This is your third try! You're missing all our activities!"

"Third? I thought you couldn't wait to go tubing," I say before I remember Daniel doesn't want to talk to me.

He shoots me an angry look, but he does answer. "Yesterday I got a cramp. Twice. I'm going to try again."

The instructor leans over and whispers something in his ear. She points at all the boys in his cabin and at the motorboat and the canoes, but Daniel shakes his head.

"I want to do the Cedar Swim," he says angrily.

So he and Anne head down the dock as Gabby and I go out in a motorboat with Ella, Isabelle, and four boys from Daniel's cabin.

Gabby and I get to go first. The inner tube is big enough to hold two. We lie on our stomachs and grab on to the handles.

"You give the thumbs-up to the boat," I tell her. "I don't want to let go."

Gabby doesn't say anything, but I feel her arm move, and within seconds we are off. The tube bumps over the waves, and water sprays our faces, and I'm holding on as tight as I can and screaming at the top of my lungs. At first it reminds me of the roller coaster. I cover my mouth with my hand.

Gabby leans into me and forces me to lean over, too. The next thing I know, the inner tube is sliding and bumping over the water all the way to the right. Then Gabby leans the other way and pulls my arm so I will follow. Now we're sliding all the way to the left. The water sprays us from all directions, and we're zooming fast. It's not at all like the roller coaster. When I was on the roller coaster, I kept thinking I would crash and die. On the inner tube, I feel extra alive. The lake and the air and the whole world are rushing into me, filling me with energy. It's the best feeling ever! When we've finally gone all around the lake, the motorboat slows down and our ride is over.

I roll on my back and scream, "That was *me-shuggeneh!*"

Gabby raises an eyebrow at me.

"Crazy," I tell her. "That was crazy!"

"I-it w-was awesome," she says.

I agree.

I wish I could tell Maya about tubing, tell her that it is my favorite thing about camp so far, but I wonder if she would even care. She said I would know that she was thinking about me all the time, but all I know is that I'm thinking about *her* and she's not here. I don't understand it. Strangers are sending me presents, but my real sister doesn't care at all. Well, if Maya doesn't care about me, then I won't care about her. That's my new sister motto.

When we get to lunch, I'm starving, but when our cabin is called to get in the lunch line, I don't hurry off like Reese, Ella, Isabelle, Lily, and Gabby. They haven't served anything I like so far.

I doubt that's going to change. You can't change who you are and you can't change what they serve for lunch at camp. That's my mess-hall motto.

Here are the foods they serve at camp that I like: nothing.

Here are the foods they serve at camp that I don't like: everything.

I really miss my mom's grilled cheese sandwiches. I step into the line just as Daniel gets in line, too.

"Hi," I say. It's weird, but it feels sort of good to see him. I still don't like him, but he *is* a little piece of home.

"Hi," he answers.

"How was your Cedar Swim?" I ask.

He scowls. "I got another cramp, and they made me stop. I get to try again this afternoon."

"That's too bad," I say. "About the cramp, I mean. It's good that you get to try again. I guess."

From the look on Daniel's face, I'm not sure he agrees with me.

"Maybe you should forget about it," I say. "You don't want to miss any more activities."

Daniel looks at me like I'm *meshuggeneh*. "What would be the point of coming to camp if I *forget* about it?"

"There are lots of other good parts of camp," I tell him. "The activities are fun, and I bet the boys in your cabin are really nice."

We inch forward in the line and Daniel shrugs. "They're okay. They never want to hear about the Cedar Swim, though. They keep trying to convince me not to do it. They're probably jealous," he says. "Besides, you don't really believe all that stuff about camp. You hate it here."

"I—" I'm not sure what to say. I couldn't wait to go home last night, and there have been other times I've been homesick, too. But there have also been times when camp hasn't been that bad. "I don't hate all of it. I'm giving everything a fair try."

"Well, that's what I'm doing—giving the Cedar

Swim a fair try." Daniel turns to the lunch lady. "Two tofu surprises." She hands each of us a plate with tofu and vegetables in a red sauce.

"You should give tofu surprise a fair try," Daniel tells me. I sniff the plate, and the tomatoey smell almost makes me gag. But the other lunch choice is Sloppy Joes, and I don't like those, either. I take my tofu surprise and grab a cup of watery apple juice. Everyone at camp calls it Cedar Cider.

Daniel and I head back to our own tables without talking.

I am the only person at my table who didn't get a Sloppy Joe.

I put a small piece of tofu on my fork and close my eyes. Here goes nothing. I take a bite and start to chew.

Reason number one that I should never have given tofu a fair try: The tofu feels like a slimy mush in my mouth. I thought tofu would be chewy, but it is slippery, like thick pudding.

Reason number two that I should never have given tofu a fair try: I can't make myself swallow it, but I don't want to spit it out in front of everyone, either. So I have to just sit there with a mouth full of yuckiness.

Soon everyone at my table is looking at me with a grossed-out expression. Their expressions must match the one on my face. Finally Gabby grabs my napkin and holds it up to my mouth. I quickly take it from her and spit out my food. My cabinmates look more disgusted than ever.

Some things don't deserve a fair try. That's my tofu motto.

I take a big gulp of Cedar Cider and try to wash the bad taste out of my mouth. Gabby pushes her plate over to me, offering to share her Sloppy Joe.

"No thank you," I whisper.

"Sami!" Becca slaps her hand down on the table and at first I think she's mad, but when I look up, she's smiling. "You just reminded me of two very important things I forgot to tell you guys!

First, don't eat anything with the word 'surprise' in the name! And second, if you don't like what's being served, there is a peanut butter and jelly station in the corner."

Becca points all the way to the other side of the mess hall, and I see a table with loaves of bread and jars of jam and peanut butter.

"Do you want to go make a PB and J?" Yael asks me.

I nod and jump up from the table. A peanut butter sandwich sounds perfect! It's one of my eleven foods! Hooray for peanut butter. That's my lunch motto.

"Can I go, too?" Isabelle asks. "I don't like Sloppy Joes, either."

Isabelle and I start walking to the peanut butter and jelly table when we hear someone behind us shout, "Wait!" It's Lily.

"I'm so glad you spit out your lunch," she tells me. "I did not want to eat that Sloppy Joe! And I'm starving. I've barely eaten anything so far."

"Me neither," says Isabelle. "I was just going to eat the top of the bun. I'm used to it. I'm a really picky eater."

"Me too," I say.

"We can be the picky eaters club," says Lily. "We can call ourselves the PB and J bunch."

We get to the table and start making our sandwiches. Lily spreads the thinnest possible layer of both peanut butter and grape jelly. Isabelle uses lots of jelly and almost no peanut butter, and my sandwich is plain peanut butter.

"Do you guys want to hear the picky eaters' song I just wrote for us?"

"You just wrote another song?" Isabelle asks me.

"Right now in your head?" Lily bugs her eyes out like she can't believe it.

I start to feel a little embarrassed but I nod. "Uh-huh."

"Cool," they both say. So I sing for them. It's to the tune of "Twinkle, Twinkle, Little Star."

73

"Picky eaters, don't you frown
Just because tofu's around.
You don't have to eat that food,
Even if they say it's good.
Peanut butter saves the day.
Three new friends all say, 'Hooray!'"

"I love it!" says Lily.

We start walking back to our table, singing our song together, when I notice Daniel watching me from his cabin's table. Everyone else at his table is sitting at one end, but Daniel is on the other side, separate. He points to my sandwich and shakes his head.

I shrug and sing a little louder. I don't think Daniel and I have the same definition of *fair try*.

CHAPTER 6

**BRING YOUR WINTER
COAT TO THE
SHOWER HOUSE**

The afternoon is just as busy with activities as the morning. Then, suddenly, at three thirty, everything stops. The whole camp gets ready for Shabbat. Yael and Becca tell us to gather our shower buckets, because we are going to the shower house. It's really crowded and we have to stand in line for a turn to shower. It seems like everyone in the entire camp is taking a shower at the same time.

When it's finally my turn, I step into the shower stall and get hit with a blast of icy water. I shriek and turn the dial all the way to hot, but the temperature doesn't change.

"I can't figure out how to make it warm!" I shout.

"You can't," Yael calls back. "Not with so many people showering. Just wash fast and try not to stand directly in the spray."

When everyone in my cabin has finished showering, and we are all standing, shivering and dripping, in our flip-flops, we walk back to the cabin.

Okay, I gave camp showers a fair try. I don't like them. Neither do the rest of my cabinmates. We have a contest to decide whose teeth are chattering loudest on the walk back from the shower house.

"Sami! Write us a cold-shower song," Lily says.

I think for a minute, then come up with one to the tune of "It's Raining, It's Pouring."

"I'm icy, I'm freezing,
I'm so cold that I'm wheezing.
My toes are numb, my brain turned dumb.
That shower wasn't pleasing."

Everyone sings it with me the rest of the way, even Gabby. She adds a loud *"Brrrr!"* at the end. We all pretend to shiver and shake when we sing it. After a few rounds, I don't even feel that cold anymore.

When we get back to our cabin, there is a giant sign hanging from the railing of our porch. It's written in rainbow lettering and has a glitter star border.

SHABBAT SHALOM, CABIN SHEMESH!
FROM YOUR FAIRY CAMPMOTHERS

The fairy campmothers again. I wonder if I will ever figure out who they are.

We walk past the sign into the cabin, and on each of our beds is another present: a tiny clay Star of David painted blue and white and hung on a blue ribbon.

"Wow!" says Reese. "That's so nice! Is this from our fairy campmothers, too?"

"Yep," Becca says. "You'll get to meet them soon."

"Let's all wear our necklaces, then!" Ella says. "They're so pretty."

Everyone agrees, and they tie the ribbons onto one another's necks. Then they put on their dresses, but I sit down on my bed.

Shabbat has started. Maya said she'd be back by Shabbat. She said she'd come see me. She *promised*.

Everyone is so busy getting dressed they don't even notice I'm still in my bathrobe—everyone but Gabby. She sits down on my bed and asks, "*F-farshtinkener?*"

I shake my head. Not even that can cheer me up today.

She points to the necklace in my hands, and then she points to my neck.

"I don't feel like wearing it," I tell her. I'd rather have my sister than a necklace.

Gabby puts her arm around my shoulders

and leans her head against mine. She doesn't try to cheer me up or tell me to feel differently, but after a while I feel better—better enough to get dressed, at least. I put on my blue sundress, and Gabby ties on my necklace and says, "M-my s-sister is h-homesick, t-too."

"You have a sister at camp?" I ask her.

She nods.

"But why hasn't she come to say hello?"

"C-camping t-trip," Gabby explains.

"Oh," I say, and I start to get a funny feeling at the edges of my brain, but before I can figure out what it is, I hear singing. It's very soft, but I know I'm not imagining it, because Reese and Ella both say, "What's that?" and run outside.

I can't hear the words of the song, but the melody is beautiful. I go out onto the front porch of the cabin with Gabby to see who's singing.

There is a parade of girls walking down the line of cabins toward us. They are all dressed up, linked arm in arm. Their song is just nonsense sounds, "*Yi-di di-dah-di-di, yi-di di-dah-di-di, yi-di di-dah-di-di-diii*," but it is sweet and happy. After I've heard it twice, I can't help singing along. Gabby sings, too.

As I watch the girls go by, I finally see Maya. She's here at camp, but she never came to say hi. She's got her arm around a girl with wavy blond hair, and they both wave at me as they walk past. I turn away, ignoring them, but I see Gabby waving back at them. She must think they were waving at her. I don't have the heart to tell her the truth.

When the end of the parade passes our cabin, Yael says, "Come on!"

We follow her down off the porch and join the parade. We keep singing as we walk to a place just past the swimming area. It looks like an outdoor theater. There are rows and rows of benches built into the side of a hill, and when we sit in them, we are looking down at a small platform on the beach of Cedar Lake. Behind it the water glows orange and pink in the sunset.

"Wow," I whisper to myself.

Down on the platform two girls light the Shabbat candles and sing the blessing. Their voices soar over us, and I think if I ever became a sleepaway camp kind of kid, I'd like to get a turn to do that. Another girl steps onto the platform and begins to sing the prayers welcoming the Sabbath Bride. The whole camp joins in, and it's like I can feel the vibrations of the songs deep in my heart.

After the sun has set and services are over, we walk toward the mess hall for dinner. Behind me, I hear someone call my name.

"Sami!"

I turn around and my cabin walks on without me. Maya runs over and wraps me in a huge hug. At first I lean my head against her, but then she says, "So are you totally a Cedar Lake girl now?"

I stiffen my spine and press my lips together.

Streams of kids are walking past us, and I don't want to cry or yell in front of them.

"I'm so excited to see you!" my sister goes on, stepping back to look at me. "I can't wait to hear how much you love camp! What have you done so far? Did you meet Gabby?"

I wonder how Maya knows Gabby, but I don't want to talk to her. I think up a song to the tune of "Row, Row, Row Your Boat."

Go, go, go away,
I don't want to talk.
You broke all your promises.
Now go take a walk.

"What's wrong?" she asks when I don't answer. "Did something happen?"

I fold my arms across my chest and glare at her.

"Sami! Please tell me. I can't help make it better if you won't tell me. I want you to love camp. Whatever it is, I'm sure it can be fixed. I promise."

It's dark and quiet where we are now. The rest of camp is in the mess hall. I can see the lights glowing in the distance and smell the chicken soup. My stomach rumbles. Chicken soup is one of my eleven foods.

I want to believe what Maya is saying, but I can't. I can't believe any of her promises anymore. I turn and run away from her as fast as I can. I hear her calling my name, but I don't stop until I get back to the amphitheater. I hide behind the last bench and see Maya down below, but she can't see me. It's really dark back here by the trees. She calls my name a couple more times, then turns and walks away.

When I'm sure she's not coming back, I climb out from behind the bench and dust off my knees. I don't know what to do next. I sit down on the bench to figure it out when I hear a noise behind me. I jump, then notice Daniel sitting at the end of the row. Oh great. I bet he's going to tell on me for hiding from Maya.

I wait for him to start lecturing me, but he just turns away and hunches his back.

I get up and walk over to him. He won't look at me.

"Daniel? Are you okay?"

He shrugs.

"Me neither," I say.

He looks up at me and scowls. "Your problems are easy, Samantha. All you have to do is try new foods."

"Daniel, sometimes you are such a *nudnik*!"

He looks shocked. I know Grandma would be angry if she heard what I just said, but I can't help myself. "If you paid attention for one second, you'd know that my name is Sami, that Maya likes her cabinmates better than her own sister, and that there is a lot more to do at camp than the Cedar Swim!"

Daniel opens his mouth to say something, but

down at the bottom of the amphitheater, Yael calls out, "Sami and Daniel, there you are!" She climbs to the top of the benches and a mixture of anger and relief is on her face. "You guys can't disappear like that. Both your cabins were searching for you. They were so worried."

"Yeah," Daniel mumbles sarcastically. "I'm sure. My cabin was probably happy they didn't have to hear about the Cedar Swim anymore."

Yael looks like she doesn't know what to say.

"I'm sorry," I tell her. "I didn't mean to make anyone worry."

She gives me a big hug. "You can always come talk to me if there is a problem," she says. "That's what I'm here for. I'll do anything I can to help."

I nod, but I don't think there is anything she can do. I just have to wait it out until it's time to go home.

"Come on. Let's go to dinner," Yael says.

She puts her arm around my shoulders, and Daniel follows us back to the mess hall. When we get there, my cabinmates jump up and surround me with hugs.

"Sami, where were you?" Reese asks.

"We were so worried!" Lily says.

"We made you a PB and J," Isabelle adds.

"Just in case you don't like chicken noodle soup," Ella explains.

Gabby holds my hand tightly like she doesn't ever want to let go.

A lump fills my throat. "I'm sorry, you guys! I didn't mean to scare you."

"Are y-you okay?" Gabby asks.

I take a deep breath.

Reason number one that I guess I am okay: My cabinmates are really, really nice. Maybe I'm not a sleepaway camp kind of kid, but the girls in my cabin are true friends, and I can't feel sad when I'm with them.

Reason number two that I guess I am okay: I am going to eat three bowls of chicken noodle soup.

"I am okay," I tell them.

We sit down at our table for dinner, and I can't believe it, but a new beginning to my Camp Cedar Lake song pops into my head. I sing the words silently.

Camp Cedar Lake,
So far away,
A home away from home.
With all your friends at Cedar Lake
You never feel alone.

Howie leads the camp in the blessing over the challah, and Yael passes the bread around the table for each of us to rip off a piece. I dip mine in my soup, and the broth is rich and tasty. The noodles are perfect, too, and the matzo balls are fluffy, just like I like them. Everyone at our table takes a turn talking about her favorite camp moments so far. It reminds me of home. At our family Shabbat dinners, my parents, Maya, and I always take turns talking about our favorite parts of the week.

After dinner, Howie stands up and starts singing a slow song in a voice that sounds almost like whining. It makes me think the song might be hundreds of years old. Lots of campers join in, and as they move through the verses, the song gets faster and faster. Soon all the campers are up out of their seats, singing and dancing around the room. When that song is over, we sing another and another, until finally I'm so tired I think I might fall asleep at my table.

Across the mess hall, Maya catches my eye and waves at me. I'm not sure what to do. I don't feel so mad anymore, but I don't know what I feel. The new beginning to my camp song pops into my head again.

With all your friends at Cedar Lake
You never feel alone.

The words I just made up confuse me. I'm not a sleepaway camp kind of kid. So why would I sing a song like that?

People should only sing songs that make sense. That's my singing motto.

CHAPTER 7

**TRY THE
SPECIAL SOUP**

When we wake up on Saturday morning, the first words out of Lily's mouth are "I can't believe mini-camp is more than halfway over!"

"Don't say that!" Ella says. "You're going to make me sad."

"M-me t-too!" Gabby adds.

"No way," Becca says. "You guys are going to have too much fun today to be sad."

"Besides," Yael says, "guess what they serve for breakfast on Saturdays?"

"Doughnuts!" I shout, because that's definitely something Maya told me about. Doughnuts are absolutely one of my eleven foods. All foods with holes in the middle are delicious. That's my breakfast motto.

"Yum!" says Isabelle. "I'll eat that."

We walk down to the mess hall arm in arm and Reese says, "Sami, sing us a doughnut song."

I think for a second, then start to sing to the tune of "I Have a Little Dreidel."

> *"I want to eat a doughnut*
> *With sprinkles on the top.*
> *But if you have no sprinkles,*
> *I'll take a choc-o-late."*

I pronounce *chocolate* like "choc-o-laaht" to make it rhyme, and we all start giggling and singing the song together.

After breakfast, Cabin Shemesh and Cabin Kochavim have to sit in the grass for a talk with Rabbi Joe. I'm ready for another hour of itchy *tukhus*, but Rabbi Joe says, "If anyone wants to grab a sweatshirt or blanket to sit on, I'll wait." He spreads his own blanket on the ground.

About half of us jump up and run to get sweatshirts and blankets, and when we return, Rabbi Joe is smiling and humming softly to himself. We sit back down, and he says, "Is everyone comfortable?"

He looks around the group, waiting for everyone to nod or say yes. Then he says, "Good. I want to tell you a story."

He pauses for a moment, then begins.

"Some of you may have heard a story called *The Sabbath Spice.*"

Some kids nod, but some kids shake their heads.

"In that story," Rabbi Joe explains, "there is a king who, one Shabbat, tastes the most delicious soup at the home of a poor peasant. The king gets the recipe so his royal chef can recreate the soup, but he cannot. Very upset, the king yells at the peasant for giving him a fake recipe, but the peasant explains that the king was missing one very special ingredient: Shabbat. From that day on, the king celebrates Shabbat before eating his soup, and the soup always tastes delicious.

"Years go by and the king is very happy, but then he hears rumors of the poor peasant's daughter. The daughter, these rumors say, serves a soup even more delicious than her father's. So the king sends a message to the peasant's daughter to expect him for dinner on Friday night.

"Friday night after services, the king goes to the peasant's daughter's home. The house is packed with people. The king has to sit crowded between an old man who speaks IN A VERY LOUD VOICE and a young boy with a runny nose. *Humph*, thinks the king, *she knew I was coming! She shouldn't have invited so many other guests.*

"The king feels so insulted he wants to leave, but then he notices a delicious aroma filling the air. The soup! The king stays. As the bowls of soup are passed around the table, each person smiles and speaks to their neighbor.

"'SHABBAT SHALOM,' the old man says loudly to the king as he hands him a bowl of soup.

"'I like your crown,' the young boy says to the king as the boy takes the bowl of soup.

"'Thank you,' the king says to them both. Each time a new bowl gets passed down, another comment is made. Soon the king knows that the old man has seventeen grandchildren and the young boy has excellent fashion sense.

"Finally the king receives his own bowl of soup. He tastes it. The broth is rich and savory with just a hint of salt and fresh herbs. The matzo balls are a perfect blend of fluffy and dense. It truly is the best soup he has ever tasted. Before he leaves, the king makes sure his royal chef gets the recipe from the peasant's daughter."

Rabbi Joe stops and smiles at each of us. "Does anyone have a prediction about what is going to happen?" he asks.

I lean over to Gabby, since we're sharing a blanket, and whisper, "The soup isn't going to taste good."

Gabby nods. She lifts my hand into the air, and Rabbi Joe points to me and says, "Yes, the girl in the *Fiddler on the Roof* T-shirt, my favorite musical."

"I think the soup isn't going to taste as good," I tell him.

"Ah," he says. "I think you're right. The next Friday night, the king returns to his quiet castle after services and settles down at his roomy table. For the first time, his dining room feels too big rather than luxurious, but he shrugs it off and dips his spoon into his bowl.

"The king closes his eyes and takes a bite, ready to savor the most delicious soup. And the soup does taste good. But no better than his usual Sabbath soup, not nearly as good as the soup at the peasant's daughter's house.

"Well, the king has been through this before.

He knows he must be missing a secret ingredient, but he can't figure out what it is. It can't be Shabbat. He's already celebrating Shabbat.

"Does anyone know what it is?" Rabbi Joe asks the group.

"The old man," says a boy from Daniel's cabin.

"The peasant's daughter," says Isabelle. "The king needs to marry her and make her the queen."

"Those are both great ideas," says Rabbi Joe. "Let's finish the story and see if you are right. Where was I?"

Rabbi Joe looks around as if he's trying to find himself. Then he looks into his lap, pats his legs, and says, "Oh, right here! The next day the king returns to the peasant's daughter and asks her to tell him the secret of the soup. 'Why is it that when I sat at your crowded, humble table, the soup tasted better than when I sat at my large and elegant dining table alone?'

"'Why, Your Majesty,' says the peasant's daughter, 'you've already answered your own

97

question. When you ate at my house, you gave others the pleasure of your friendship and accepted theirs in return. When you ate in your palace, you kept yourself apart from all who would love you.'

"The king sees that the peasant's daughter is telling the truth, and from that day on, every Friday night the king invites the old man and the young boy and everyone in the kingdom to a feast of chicken, vegetables, conversation, and, of course, the most delectable soup in all the land."

When Rabbi Joe finishes his story, he sits quietly for a minute and smiles at us.

"Does anyone have any thoughts they want to share about that story?" Rabbi Joe asks.

No one raises their hand.

"Or thoughts about anything?" Rabbi Joe adds with a laugh.

Still no one raises their hand. I look around and see that most people are keeping their eyes on the grass. Then Gabby raises her right hand.

Rabbi Joe calls on her, and as she looks

around the group and notices everyone's stares, she freezes. I squeeze her other hand.

"I-i-it's l-like c-camp," she says. "B-being with f-friends. It m-m-makes everything n-nicer."

Rabbi Joe beams at Gabby, and she squeezes my hand back.

Then Daniel raises his hand. "That doesn't make sense," he says. "It's impossible. Soup can't taste different just because of a day of the week or people. Those things aren't *in* the soup."

Rabbi Joe nods. "You're right, Daniel. The soup probably did taste exactly the same each time. I bet the king only *thought* it tasted different."

Daniel nods, but then Rabbi Joe keeps talking.

"There are many, many wonderful things in the world," he tells us. "But without the people we love, without our friends and family, are those things really as good as we thought they were?"

I think about Rabbi Joe's words. Tubing was

fun, but it was more fun because I was with Gabby. My peanut butter sandwich tasted better because of the picky eaters club. Even a cold shower wound up being fun when I sang about it with my cabin.

And then I think of Maya. I thought camp was less fun because she wasn't with me. But maybe camp was less fun because I was angry at her.

I look over at Daniel, sitting off to the side by himself. He's spent all his time trying to do the Cedar Swim. Alone. Maybe that's why he doesn't think the soup would taste any different. He's never even tried the other kind of soup.

And he thinks *I'm* the picky eater!

CHAPTER 8

**ALWAYS GO TO
FREE SWIM**

After our talk with Rabbi Joe, I ask Yael if I can go visit my sister. She says yes, so I run to Maya's cabin. But it's empty. My shoulders sink, and I sit down on the steps of her front porch, wondering where she can be. Just then, the girl with blond wavy hair, the one Maya had her arm around in the parade, walks up to the cabin.

"Hi," she says, smiling. She reminds me of someone, but I can't figure out who. "You're Sami, right?"

I nod.

"I'm Carly," she says. "My cabin's doing a

nature walk, but I forgot to put on bug spray." She runs inside to get some. When she comes back out, she sits down next to me.

I shoo a fly away from my face. "I was looking for my sister."

"She really wants to talk to you," Carly says. "But she doesn't want to make you upset."

I really want to talk to her, too. "I'm not upset anymore."

Carly takes a deep breath. "That's good. I felt so bad when you were sad. You and Maya have helped me so much. I was really homesick, and Maya was the only person who could make me forget about it. She taught me your silly song. It was the first time I laughed at camp. You've been really great for Gabby, too."

"Gabby?" I ask. I suddenly realize who Carly is. "You're Gabby's sister."

"Yeah," she says, laughing. "Didn't you know that?"

I shake my head. "But I haven't done any-

thing for Gabby. She's the one who keeps help-
ing me."

Carly shrugs. "All I know is that she doesn't
talk if she isn't comfortable, and here she's talking all the time. I think that's because of you."

"But I didn't *do* anything," I say. "I didn't know
what to do."

"You were her friend. That's way better than
doing something," Carly says. Then she stands
up. "I better go, or they'll be so far along the path
I'll never find them."

"Tell Maya I stopped by to say hi," I say as she
leaves.

"I will," she says. "She'll be so happy. She can't
wait to hear about mini-camp."

I smile. I can't wait to tell her.

That afternoon, as my cabin heads down to free
swim, I see Daniel walking to the beach alone.

Reason that I would like to ignore my cousin:
He is still a *nudnik*.

Reason that I shouldn't ignore my cousin: I guess Grandma was right. He may be a *nudnik* cousin, but he's *my nudnik* cousin.

"Daniel!" I shout, and run to catch up with him. "Are you going to free swim?"

"I'm going to do the Cedar Swim one more time," he says with a shrug.

"But you haven't tried the water trampoline," I say. "Or the Blob."

Daniel looks tempted, but he says, "It's my last chance to do the Cedar Swim."

"No," I say. "It's your last chance to have free swim."

I grab Daniel's arm and pull him down to the beach with me. "You have to try the Blob," I tell him. "It's the best."

We leave our towels in the sand, and I swim Daniel out to the puffball and show him where to sit. Gabby climbs up the platform and shouts, *"MESHUGGENEH!"* as she jumps. Daniel and I fly into the air and land in the water with a huge splash. When we come up for air, Daniel rubs his eyes and squints out at the lake.

"What?" I ask. "Do you wish you were doing the Cedar Swim?"

He shakes his head as we swim back to the Blob. "This is way better than the Cedar Swim," he admits.

I climb back onto the puffball. Gabby is still sitting where she landed. "You stay there," Daniel tells her. "This time I want to jump. Want to come?" he asks me.

I shake my head. "I don't do the jumping part," I say, looking up at the platform. It's better to fly than to jump. That's my Blob motto.

I climb next to Gabby as a boy from Daniel's cabin swims over to the platform.

"Daniel," he calls out. "I thought you weren't doing free swim."

Daniel looks down at me, then at the boy. "I changed my mind," he says. "It was my last chance."

"We're going to play Marco Polo," the boy says. "Do you want to play with us?"

"Sure," Daniel says. "I just have to finish this jump. Do you want to jump with me?"

The boy climbs up next to Daniel, and they count to three, then jump.

Gabby and I fly up in the air, and as I hit the water *tukhus*-first, I think about next summer at home. I won't get to do the Blob with Gabby again. I won't get to go tubing or sing "The Farshtinkener Song" late at night when everyone else is sleeping. I wish I knew how to turn myself into a sleepaway camp kind of kid.

I also wish I knew the Yiddish word for *wedgie*. It would sure come in handy.

That night, after my cabin eats a picnic dinner of cheese sandwiches and chips, everyone in the camp heads out to the middle of the field. We are going to make Havdalah to mark the end of the Sabbath. The sky is deep indigo blue, and the sun is just barely hanging on above the edge of Cedar Lake. I can even see a couple of stars in the sky. Stars shine so much brighter at camp than they do at home.

Rabbi Joe stands next to a table in the middle of the field, and Howie stands next to him, strumming his guitar. As the campers arrive cabin by cabin, they put their arms around one another and form a circle around Howie and Rabbi Joe. No one talks. Rabbi Joe lights a braided candle, and we all watch the flame flicker against the dark as we start to sway and sing. It's another wordless song, but this one is slower, more bittersweet, like a happy good-bye. Shabbat is over.

I put my arm around Gabby and we rock back and forth. Mini-camp is almost over, too.

My heart squeezes, but I push the thought away and keep singing.

Suddenly a person puts her arm around me on the other side. I turn to look. It's Maya.

"Hi," she says in a quiet voice, like she's

worried I'm still angry. "I've been looking for you all afternoon."

"Hi," I say back softly. "You found me."

She presses her head against mine for a second. "This is one of my favorite parts of camp," she whispers. "Isn't it peaceful?"

I nod. It's very peaceful. I could stand swaying with Maya and Gabby forever. I look at Gabby and see Carly standing on her other side. It's funny that we have sisters in the same cabin. I start to have another thought about that, but Howie changes from the wordless song to the blessings for the end of Shabbat. We sing the blessings for the candle and the wine and the spice box. Then we sing a song wishing everyone a good week.

When that's over, Maya hugs me and says, "I'm so glad you guys are wearing the stuff we made you."

She points to the friendship bracelet and the necklace, and I slap myself on the forehead.

"You guys are the fairy campmothers!" I say, looking back and forth between Maya and Carly.

They put their arms around each other. "Surprise!" they say.

Gabby puts her arm around me. "W-we're f-fairy c-camp sisters," she says.

Here is what I like about what Gabby said: It's nice to have an extra sister. That way you always have one when you need one.

I put my arm around her, too. "We're *farsh-tinkener* camp sisters," I say. Then I remember the rest of my camp sisters.

"Come on," I tell Maya and Carly. "My whole cabin wants to meet you!"

Gabby and I introduce the fairy campmothers to our cabin, and then it's time to go to bed.

It's pitch-dark outside as we walk to our cabin. The sky is filled with millions of twinkling stars. It looks like the planetarium.

Gabby grabs my arm and points. "A sh-shoot-ing star!"

I look and see a streak of light sizzle, then fade to black.

"Cool," Isabelle says.

"Make up a song, Sami," Ella says.

"Okay, but you guys have to help me." I sing the first line.

"Sizzle, sizzle, shooting star."

Gabby adds the second.

"We wish upon you from afar."

Then Lily.

"We don't want our camp to end."

And Reese.

"We will miss our brand-new friends."

Ella goes next.

"Sizzle, sizzle, shooting star."

Everyone looks at Isabelle. She scrunches up her face like she's thinking really hard. Then she sings.

"Don't eat the tofu, it will make you barf."

Everyone laughs.

"Isabelle!" Ella says.

"What?" Isabelle asks. "The last line is hardest."

"*Star* and *barf* don't even rhyme," Lily says. "And it's a song about how much we're going to miss each other."

"Oh, yeah," Isabelle says, looking sad. "Right."

"That's okay," I tell her. "You guys *were* my friends when I spit out the tofu. Even that's a good memory." When I think back on everything that's happened in the past few days, it seems like all I can remember are the good things. Is it possible that I was wrong about what kind of kid I am?

Yael and Becca walk up to our cabin, and Yael says, "Don't start getting sad over memories yet. You still have one more morning!"

"And it's the best morning yet," Becca adds. "Ropes course!"

I turn to Gabby and a shiver runs down my spine. I do not want to do ropes. She grabs my hand. "I-it w-will b-be okay," she says.

We all walk into the cabin and start getting

ready for bed. I'm confused again. Just a second ago I was starting to think that maybe I had changed. I thought maybe I had become a sleep-away camp kind of kid, but now I know that's impossible. Ropes course? No way.

CHAPTER 9

**DON'T FORGET TO
PACK YOUR COUSIN**

On the last morning of camp, we have an extra-long cabin cleanup, because we have to repack our duffel bags.

"Let's pack fast!" Becca says. "You want to have as much time as possible on the ropes course."

I walk to my cubby as slowly as I can. I pick up one T-shirt and walk back to my duffel bag. I put it inside. Then I head back to my cubby for the next T-shirt. Good packers take their time. That's my packing motto.

Pretty soon, my cabinmates are all packed up. They look at me.

"Let's help Sami finish," Becca says. Everyone rushes over to me.

"No!" I shout.

Everyone freezes. I remember when I screamed on the first day and take a deep breath.

"I mean, no thank you. You guys just go ahead. I'll catch up to you when I'm done." *When ropes course is finished,* I think.

"B-but w-we'll m-miss you," Gabby says.

"And everyone has to go to everything together," Isabelle says. "Remember?"

Yael looks at me carefully, then says, "You guys go ahead. I'll stay with Sami."

"Does that sound good to you?" Becca asks me softly.

"Yes." I am sorry that I won't get to spend the last hours of camp with my cabin, but I am glad that I won't have to do ropes.

"Pack fast," Isabelle and Reese tell me as they leave the cabin.

"Yeah," Ella says. "We need you to write a ropes song for us."

"We need our whole cabin to be together," Lily says.

"D-do you w-want me t-to stay?" Gabby asks.

I shake my head. I do want her to stay, but I don't want her to miss the ropes course. Gabby's a top bunk kind of kid. She loves being up high. Sometimes it's okay to be alone so that someone you love can do something they love. That motto works for camp sisters and real sisters. "I want you to go do ropes."

"Okay," she says, following Becca out of the cabin.

When she's gone, I walk over to my cubby, take out one more T-shirt, and put it in my duffel.

"Wow," says Yael. "You are a really neat packer."

I nod. "Yep. I don't want my T-shirts to get all wrinkled on the ride home."

"Oh," Yael says, sitting down on my bed. "I

guess I was wrong. I thought it was because you didn't want to do the ropes course."

I freeze with one hand inside my cubby.

"Because, you know," Yael says, "you don't have to do the ropes course."

A little fleck of dust floats past my nose, and I blow it away. "I thought everybody had to do everything."

Yael scratches her head. "Sort of," she says. "Everybody has to do most things, but we would never make you do something you were really scared of."

I feel so relieved. I grab everything left in my cubby and shove it into my bag in one giant pile.

"What are we waiting for, then?" I ask Yael. "Let's go!"

The ropes course is higher than high. Even though my feet are planted on the ground, just looking up at the ropes makes me feel dizzy. I sit down on a bench and hold on to it with both hands. Everyone in my cabin and Daniel's cabin is wearing a helmet and getting hooked to a safety line. They start to climb to a platform at the top of the course where they will walk across rope bridges, swing from rope swings, and slide along a zip line.

"Sami!" Reese shouts from the platform. "You made it! Come on up."

I shake my head. "I'm happy down here!" I shout back, even though I do feel a little lonely sitting all by myself.

I hear mumbling, and I can tell that all the campers on the platform are talking about me. Then one of them climbs back down. At first I'm worried it's Gabby, but it's not. It's Daniel.

At the bottom he unhooks his safety line and takes off his helmet. Then he walks over to me. Oh no. I do not want to hear his advice about how easy it will be to get over my fear of heights.

"I'm not going up there, Daniel," I tell him.

"I know," he says, plopping down on the bench next to me. "Neither am I."

"What? Why?"

"Because you're alone," he says. "And camp is about being with the people you care about."

I look at my cousin. I never thought I'd say it, but he's actually being a *mensch*.

"Sometimes you're a really nice person," I tell him.

"I know," he says, nodding.

"Besides," he adds, "do you have any idea how high that platform is? Anyone who goes on that thing is *meshuggeneh*! It's worse than the roller coasters at my birthday party."

Daniel and I both laugh.

When our cabins have finished the ropes course, it's time for us to get back on the bus to go home. This time I sit next to Gabby, and Daniel sits in the row behind us with one of the boys from his cabin.

Howie leads us in another sing-along, and Gabby and I sing at the tops of our lungs. When the sing-along is over, Howie comes to my seat

and says, "Hey, little songwriter, I've been thinking about you all weekend and wondering. Did
you change your tune?"

I nod. "I wrote new lyrics to my song," I tell
him. "Want to hear them?"

"Ab-so-lutely!" he says, and settles into the
seat across the aisle while I sing.

"Camp Cedar Lake,
So far away,
Our home away from home.
With all your friends at Cedar Lake
You'll never feel alone.
Camp Cedar Lake, Camp Cedar Lake,
Your trees so tall and free.
And all your friends at Cedar Lake
Feel just like family."

When I finish singing, Howie nods at me.
"Now, *that's* a song."

"I-it was g-great!" Gabby adds.

"Thank you," I say.

"So you have to promise me something," Howie says. "You have to promise to help me teach it to the whole camp next summer."

Next summer? My heart skips a beat, and I realize something.

I may not be a sleepaway camp kind of kid, but I *am* a Camp Cedar Lake kind of kid.

"Next summer," I say. "I promise!"

JENNY MEYERHOFF is the author of the chapter book *Third Grade Baby*, *Queen of Secrets*, and *Playing Cupid*. When Jenny was nine she went to Camp Ramah in Canada, home of the real Skeleton Lake. As far as she remembers, it was not haunted, but it was cold! Jenny now lives in Riverwoods, Illinois, with her husband and three children. Sadly, she no longer goes to summer camp. You can visit her online at jennymeyerhoff.com.